Purgatory:

A Dukes of Hell Novella

By: M Francis Lamont

COVER CREDIT:

Photography: M. Lomond

Formatting: Crys Kladreau

Dedicated to the survivors: you're strong enough.

Thank you to the friends who offered their insight, trusted me with their stories and helped me to create these new characters for the Dukes world.

Thanks to Craig for making sure I didn't betray the Dukes, even if it meant rewriting three chapters and changing the villain's backstory.

Thanks to Seamus and Bruce for the new heroes, I can't wait for them to get their own books. Chris, Tracey, and Randy, for your suggestions and Darren for your unwavering support. You guys mean the world to me.

To the Duchesses, Liz, Kat, and Jodi: A sisterhood forged in hell and bound in blood…and cheesecake. I love you.

My book team, Lila, Sara, Kerri, Steff and Hedda, you folks are amazing, and I am eternally grateful for all you help and encouragement.

For anyone who has suffered and survived the atrocities of human trafficking, I salute your bravery and your strength. You are not alone.

Trauma trigger warning: This book contains scenes of kidnapping, graphic sexual torment, and assault. Reader discretion is strongly advised.

<u>1</u>

"Are you sure you wanna go to this party Steff?" Brenna asked from the closet where she was digging for the matching vinyl pump to the one Steff was holding. "You're either going to end up pissed or pissed off."

"Yeah I wanna go and even if I didn't want to, I have to. It's the chapter anniversary and none of my brothers could make it, neither could Ox, so I gotta make an appearance at least." She adjusted her hair in the mirror and looked over at the closet. "Did you find it yet?"

"Got it." Brenna climbed out of the closet with the shoe.

"Perfect." Steff slid her feet into the bright green toed pump and pivoted to admire how it transitioned from the glittering green to the shiny black heel. "Those damn Irishmen won't know what hit 'em."

"Tell me again how this works? You're not a member of the club, but your brothers are. Somehow that means you've got to make an appearance at this party because it would be rude not to. Even though it has nothing to with you or school?"

"Something like that, yeah." Steff said, taking a deep breath. "I've gotta go, pay respects and flirt my ass off." She turned to look at her butt in the dress that had taken way more of her wardrobe budget than she wanted to admit. It was a bright emerald green silk with a layer of black sheer chiffon over it to create a shadowed effect that clung to every curve she had to work with. If it got her what she wanted tonight it'd be worth it, but damn these Boston boys were harder to crack than she had expected.

"Flirt? What about that big long-haired guy that comes around from Tennessee?" Brenna asked, sliding into her own dress. "Bear? Bull?"

"Ox?" Steff said, unable to stop the smile from spreading across her lips. "He's not actually from Tennessee but he's there right now."

"He's not? Where is he from then? Won't he mind you flirting and more if you get your way out there tonight?"

"Nah. He won't mind." Steff said, shaking her head.

The two young women grabbed their coats and headed out to Steff's 1967 Impala. As always she smiled at the sight of the shiny black car.

"Hey there Dean. Ready to go for a ride?"

It was a long running joke in her family that the only man she would ever leave Ox for completely was her favorite tv character. That was why, as a way of showing her how much he trusted her, Ox had given her the car, with a custom plate, as a present when she left Nashville to come to Harvard. Every time she saw it she thought of her big burly Ox and her panties got wet enough to change.

It was a sexy car and the man who gave it to her was even sexier.

"Seriously? He's not going to mind you going out to this place and flirting, trying to bang one of them?" Brenna asked.

Steff gunned the engine and rolled her eyes.

"Ox would be more upset if I didn't do it. He knows that no one gets me going like he does and as much fun as those Irish boys up here are he is the only man I want to keep. The rest of them are just appetizers."

"Oh my god did you seriously just call those guys appetizers?" She started to giggle.

"Yeah sure. Mozza sticks. Hard on the outside with a sticky white center."

Both girls burst out laughing while Steff shifted into gear and moved them out onto the road. She would never bring Brenna to the clubhouse in daylight, there was a bit of an unwritten rule about that kind of thing, but at night it wasn't likely that she would remember where it was and so she couldn't bring police or any other unwanted elements. Normally she wouldn't even bring a newbie like Brenna, but it wasn't the smartest idea to go to a new clubhouse alone, especially when the guys you were visiting knew exactly who you were.

The pulled up the three and a half story mansion and Steph smirked when Brenna's jaw dropped at the historic house surrounded by motorbikes. Every one of the big windows was lit up, even the top floor and the attic which both had drapes drawn so that the inside rooms were hidden. Steff could guess what was going on in those rooms.

There might not be a lot of girls in the main hall for the party, just the waitresses and a few girls that would have been invited by members or came with them, but there would be a whole other world somewhere upstairs in the house. In some of those rooms there would be deals going down that would affect more people in Boston than would ever know. Lives and livelihoods would be changed forever by people in those rooms. In other rooms there would be girls in all kinds of costumes or buck-naked selling what they had for drugs or money and there would be more men buying than the club would have found girls to sell. The game was supply vs demand and no one knew how to play it like the Dukes of Hell Club.

Ego's were bound to be on full display tonight and so she had to bring her best game-face to do the Dukes of Hell Nashville Chapter proud. There was always the chance that the local mobsters could make an appearance, the two groups had more connection through business than most people thought. There was one associate, Mic, she didn't know what his level was or what he did, but the way he watched everyone reminded Steff of Whiskey and the way he always seemed to simply know things that he shouldn't. It was a disturbing blend of sexy and creepy. With Whiskey it was sexy as hell but she didn't know Mic well enough to make a call one way or the other, but he was interesting and drank the same whiskey that Ox did, so they would definitely be buying each other a round tonight.

"This place is incredible. They really turned one of these old places into a clubhouse? Is there, like, a secret knock or something?"

"Oh good lord, Brenna. This is not a kiddy club or copycat tv show, this is a full-blown one percent club. I mean, they're fantastic and some of the best men you could know, but there is a certain element of truth to biker legends so be polite, respectful and have a fun time. Don't try to understand things or pretend that you understand things because of the tv shows you watch, okay?"

"It's gotta be a little bit like them though, right?" Brenna asked, making Steff scoff as she knocked on the door.

"Maybe just a little bit." She replied when a tall, blue-eyed man with a blonde ponytail and short, trimmed, beard opened the door. "Satan? Demoted to doorman already?"

The son of the national president laughed and ushered them both inside the house.

"Not even remotely. I was just near the door and I was lucky enough to be the one to open the door to the two prettiest girls in Boston. Who's your friend?" He looked from Steff to Brenna hungrily, the same way every member of every chapter looked right past her to any other girl in the room.

"This is my roommate Brenna." Steff waved her hand at her friend. "She is a math major and way too smart for you. Way too innocent too."

"Hey, I'm not that innocent." Brenna said, twirling a strand of her hair around while she stared up at Satan, who was grinning down at her.

Steff couldn't blame either of them. Brenna was cute and had a great rack, on top of being brilliant. She had short, red-brown hair that was soft and shiny, big brown eyes and a killer smile. Satan could have been a runway model and was easily the sexiest man she knew before she had met Ox. He was also the son of the national president, a man that her brother Blair hated more than almost anyone else and, as far as women were concerned, the most amoral womanizer in the club. She had seen him take groups of women into the bedrooms and come out hours later to take another group to a different bed.

He was an animal and, she was fairly sure, a nymphomaniac. He was also the man she had wanted to get in bed with since she was sixteen, also one of the many that didn't see her as a woman, just as 'Viper and Loch's little sister.'

It was infuriating.

"Well we'll just have to see how innocent you're not. Can I get you a drink Brenna? Gin and tonic for you Steff or are you drinking whiskey tonight with the man himself?" Satan said with that infuriatingly charming grin that drove women to distraction, and nudity.

"Whiskey's here?"

"Go see for yourself. I'll bring the drinks." Satan said, laughing as he opened the door. "Welcome to Purgatory."

Steff grinned as they stepped into the party hall. She scanned the room eagerly, looking for the bright blue eyes of Whiskey. He was the personal enforcer for the club president, Wrath, and though he treated her like a kid he was always nice to her, so was Wrath, which made no sense to her but she'd take it since it was better than being ignored.

"There they are. Come on Brenna. You gotta meet Whiskey."

She took Brenna's hand and dodged through the crowd to make her way to the grinning man with the shaved head standing next to the silver-haired daddy type who was holding court for senior members. When she got to the circle Steff cringed, Wrath's oldest friend, Machete, was on his left side with a big drink in his hand. The guy was a class one creep. He was the only guy in the club that remembered that Steff was a legal age woman and the only one that made her wish that she wasn't.

The man had to be over fifty, with more grey in his hair than the dirty blonde it had been when she was a kid. His eyes were dark, beady, rat like and shifty. He was covered in old flash tattoos that were violent and crude, he loved to tell what devious thing each piece was commemorating, especially to girls he was hitting on.

Steff didn't know anyone that had gone to bed with him without being compensated for it. He was simply too creepy. Most of the girls that worked for the club would come out of the bedroom bloodied and bruised, crying and needing time off to heal.

Once, Loch had caught him trying to hit on her. He broke his finger punching Machete and told Steff if he ever caught her talking with him again he would send her out of the country. Viper had, of course, agreed with him because that was before Jade and the two of them had been inseparable then. Now the whole family was divided, and she was in the middle and all alone most of the time. There was no one here to keep her safe from the monsters anymore, except for Ox.

"Hey Whiskey." Steff said with a smile, stepping into the circle to accept a hug from the gruff, bearded man. "It's been a while. You still drinking single malt? Satan said he'd bring a round over."

"Yeah, sure kiddo. Thanks for that and for bringing a bit of company with you too."

"Not a kid." Steff elbowed him and turned to the president. "Hello Wrath. I didn't know that you were coming."

"Good evening, Steffany." He replied, standing up to give her a hug. "How many times do I need to tell you to just call me Sam? You here alone tonight?"

"I couldn't call you that. It would be disrespectful. I told you before that my brothers schooled me on how to behave around members ever since I can remember. I know the rules and know how to address the man in the room." Steff said with a cocky grin.

"Not the only man in the room, Steffy." Machete said, standing up to slide his arm across her shoulder. "Who's your little friend?"

"It's Steff, or Steffany. Not Steffy." She said, sliding out from underneath his arm with a shudder that she didn't bother to repress. "My roommate from school isn't here for entertainment. She's here to make sure that I get home safe after representing for Nashville since no one from home could make it out."

"Well now that just isn't true sweetheart." He said with a grin that made Steff nauseous. "Didn't you see Dagger at the bar talking to the devil?"

<u>**2**</u>

Steff turned to see where Machete was looking and tried not to groan out loud when she saw the lieutenant of the Nashville chapter, Dagger, doing shots with Satan.

"Oh shit. Well I guess I didn't need to get all dressed up and come out here after all." Steff said with a shrug. Turning her head to look at Brenna she saw that her friend was staring around the room at the men in various leather vests. "Maybe we can stick around for a little while though? If that's alright with you Wrath?"

The president stood up and wrapped his arms around her in another warm hug.

"You are always welcome in my house Steff. My son will see that you're taken care of." Wrath looked at the golden god walking towards them with his hands full of drinks. "Boy, see that these two young ladies have a good night and get home safe. Remember what I said, don't disappoint me."

He gave Brenna a smile, nodded to her then dropped a kiss to Steff's cheek.

"Have fun kids. I have a meeting upstairs."

Steff watched a path clear in front of the leading man in the room, wondering what it is that he had warned Satan about until he pressed a drink into her hand and said quietly in her ear.

"Impressive, isn't he? I'll never have that kind of affect on these guys but it's great to see the respect they have for him."

"Yeah." Steff agreed, taking a sip. "You never know, you might find your own way to inspire that kind of respect and loyalty. What did he warn you about though?"

"Nothing serious." Satan shrugged; his eyes glued to Brenna's tits that looked as though they were going to pop out of her top any second. "Just that no one here is allowed to fuck you and you're to be taken home safe before the hard partying starts."

"What? Hell no. I don't care what rules he gave you. If I want to get some I will. I'm a damn adult and no one is in charge of my sex-life but me." Steff growled, slamming back the double of whiskey. "Don't seduce my room-mate though, her parents would kill her for getting involved with one of you guys."

"So, you're in charge of your sex life, and hers?" A teasing Irish lilt said from behind her. "Sounds like Tennessee to me."

"Mic!" Steff spun and threw her arms around the mobster standing in front of her. His strong arms wrapped around her in a warm hug. "Let me look at you. Is it just me or are you more handsome than I remember?"

"It's just the luck of Irish, and the new suit doesn't hurt either."

It certainly didn't hurt the thug's sex appeal, which was already strong enough. Steff dragged her eyes from his buffed black boots up the charcoal grey pants and let her eyes linger for just a minute too long on his belt buckle, wondering if the rumors about him were true.

She'd heard that he was hung like a horse and fucked like an Olympian, the Greek kind, not the ones in spandex. There was a rumor about him and a weekend with the daughter of the president, of the country not the club, but she thought that was too bizarre to be true. She had also heard that he wasn't allowed back in Ireland because he'd slept with the wife of the wrong man. That as more likely, so was the one about him running a hit squad, but that didn't concern her too much tonight.

From the waist up he looked every bit the stereotypical Irish mobster. With a crisp black shirt, straining across his biceps as he drank, over a tank-top so white it had to be new tucked into his waist that was not thin but was certainly solid muscle. The suspenders he wore would have had an aging affect on someone like Blades or even Wrath, but on Mic they gave him almost a prohibition era look.

It was the newsboys cap pulled low over his blue eyes that completed the look for Steff though. He looked so damn good that it wouldn't take much of the whiskey that he, Whiskey and Steff were all drinking to convince her to go upstairs to one of the private rooms to find the truth about every one of those rumors.

"It sure doesn't hurt one little bit. I wonder how lucky the Irish really are tonight?" She said with a smile, running her hand suggestively up his arm to grip the muscle underneath.

"Oh I'm feeling pretty lucky there Tennessee." He said, looking down at her hungrily.

"You'll be even luckier if you remember the rules about touching that girl." Whiskey said with a growl while Satan walked towards the pool tables with Brenna on his arm.

"Shut up Whiskey. I am not a baby and I'm not your sister. If I want to spend some time alone with Mic I will do just that. He's not a member and you can't tell him what to do." Steff snapped, glaring at the enforcer.

She was tired of being treated as less than any other girl simply because she was related to a few of the members. She was just as pretty, just as desirable and, damnit, tonight she'd feel like it.

"Steff?" Mic said, sliding an arm around her waist. "You want to go somewhere and talk about this?"

"No Mic, I want to go upstairs and fuck your brains out."

He didn't say a word just arched an eyebrow and led her upstairs, leaving a visibly annoyed Whiskey behind them.

Steff would make amends with him later, right now she wanted to feel like more than a child. Ignoring a few gawking stares from the Boston Members she led Mic to one of the bedrooms left unlocked for use during parties. There was a large bed with plain blankets and uncomfortable looking pillows. It obviously wasn't intended for anyone to sleep in here, simply use the space for a bit of carnal fun then pop back down to whatever party was going on. Just like she was going to do with Mic who was leaning against the closed door and watching her carefully.

"What do you really want up here Steff? Make a few of the boys jealous? Or just get away from Dagger?" He said, crossing his arms over his broad chest. "Tell me."

Steff knew that beneath the suit shirt Mic's arms were tattooed, but unlike a club member he would rarely show them off. They meant something far more personal to his kind of man than the ones that she was related to who got them on whim more often than not. She would know each of Mic's intimately by the end of the night, commit each mark to memory. There was something about him that made her feel comfortable and excited all at the same time. There didn't need to be awkwardness between them unless he made it that way.

"I want to get away from Dagger and Machete. I could have done that by leaving, though if Dagger's here then there is no need for me to be, other than to have fun." She stepped towards him with a smile. "Do you want to have fun with me Mic?"

"Darlin' girl, the fun I could have with you would turn that pretty little head right around." Mic said in his Irish lilt, standing up straight and prowling towards her. "You sure you want to play my kind of games?"

Steff felt a shiver go right up her spine. In this moment, everything about him screamed predator and common sense told her to run, but she couldn't. She was mesmerized by his blue eyes and when he touched her cheek she thought her knees were going to melt.

"Mic, I brought you up here. I meant what I said." She said, trying to sound as confident as she wanted to me.

"Then why're you backing away, sweetheart?" He asked when she tripped and found herself sitting on the edge of the bed. "Looking a little scared there. Not too late to back out, kid."

He would let her, of course, and no one would ever know what happened up here. Steff knew if she backed out there would never be a chance with him again.

"I'm not a kid Mic." She said, staring up at him through her lashes.

"Oh really?" He teased with a grin, reaching out to touch her cheek again.

"Yeah. Really." She replied, reaching to unfasten his belt.

It might be considered forward or skanky in any other circle but as she tugged his cock free of his pants and flicked her tongue across the tip she knew it was all but expected by any other girl but her. Even Brenna would probably be doing something similar by the end of the night and she'd bust balls if it was Satan or Whiskey.

"You sure you're not a kid? You're licking that thing like it's some kind of lolly." He said, sliding his fingers into her hair.

Steff's response was wordless but spoke volumes none the less. Wrapping her lips around his shaft she sucked him hard to the back of her throat. They were moving together so smoothly she couldn't tell if he was thrusting into her mouth, letting her set the rhythm herself, or moving her head with the hand that was gripping her head tight. It was hot and the growl coming from his lips was soaking her skirt.

She was ready for this and so was he. Every time she buried her nose in the trimmed curls at the base of his cock she could feel the way his body tightened. Maybe the men around here didn't see her as a kid after all. Not all of them anyway.

"Fuck." He murmured, pulling back from her mouth. "You are way too good at that for being a kid. Where did you learn that kind of thing?"

"Call me kid again and you'll never know." She said with a smile, leaning back on her elbows and looking up from the bed. "The question is, what can you do that I haven't already tried?"

"That you haven't already tried?" He asked, unbuttoning his shirt, and tossing it to the chair beside him. "Cheeky little brat, aren't you?"

"You have no idea."

Steff was doing her best not to let herself get distracted by the patterns of knotwork that crept from his shoulder across his pecs and down his ribs, but it was hard. So were his abs and his cock that was still glistening from being in her mouth.

"Come a little closer though and I'll see what I can do to give you an idea."

"I think I'm the one that's going to be giving the lessons tonight." Mic said, moving onto the bed and creeping towards her. "The first of which is that good little girls take their clothes off before they get into bed with boys. So, strip. Now."

She squealed with delight when Mic grabbed the shoe that had been buried in the closet and tossed it over his shoulder, followed by the one that had been under the bed.

"Why would I do that when you're doing such a great job undressing me and I can just lay here, being tugged, and tossed around, by a sexy Irishman?"

"You'll do it because I'm telling you to."

"And?" She shivered with a delicious taste of fear in her mouth.

"No 'and'. Just do it. Because you want to, so you'll do it now."

<u>**3**</u>

He simply lay there next to her, watching her trying to decide what she was going to do. Any other man, even Ox, she would have been worried that he was going to think that she was second guessing her desire or his intention. Mic was just calmly waiting for her to comply with his command, as if he knew that she was going to do it, simply because he said so.

Rising to her knees Steff lifted the hem of her dress. Pulling it slowly up her body she paused with a smile when she heard his sharp intake of breath when he saw the black lace thong she was wearing underneath the silk dress. There was no faking the desire in that sound and when she pulled the dress over her head, revealing the matching French-cut bra that held her breasts like a scoop of ice-cream in a fancy little dish, she couldn't help her smile when their eyes met.

"You're staring, Mic." She said, resting back on her heels. Running the tip of her finger from her knee up her torso to zig zag over the curve of her breasts. "See something you like?"

"I see everything I like. Get over here."

He gave her a brief curl of her finger summoning her to crawl across the mattress until she was poised above him.

"Everything?" She purred, flicking her tongue across her lips.

"Damn right." He growled, digging his fingers into her hair, and pulling her down into a kiss so hot that it would have sent her to her knees if she weren't already on them. "Every single thing I can see, touch, taste. I like it all."

He moved his kiss from her lips to her ear and down her neck while his hands began to wander over her skin. Steff closed her eyes, pressed a kiss to the top of his head and surrendered to every sensation his touch was bringing to her starved nerves. His hand on her breast was firm but not hard, with just enough pressure to let her know that he was in control but not cause her pain. It was magic and exactly what she needed.

It had been months since she had seen Ox and she needed this. Even though the polyamorous nature of their relationship meant that she could have a college boyfriend or even date one of the Boston members, there hadn't been anyone she liked well enough to even try with that didn't treat her like a child. Mic was different though. This wasn't going to be dating, probably wasn't going to be anything other than friendship beyond tonight, but damn it felt so good when he sucked her nipple between his teeth.

When he kissed her mouth, it tasted like whiskey and she forgot about proving anything to her brothers. When he pressed himself against her thigh she forgot that she had come here to prove a point and lost herself in the feeling that his fingers between her legs created. He teased and played her nerves to arousal and set her senses singing. He was playing her body like a fiddle and she loved it. She hadn't felt so alive, desired, since the last time she had been in Ox's arms months ago.

She needed this, badly.

"Mic…" She whispered, dragging her fingers up his back while he peppered her stomach with soft kisses and sharp nips and bites. "More. I need more. Please."

"You want more? Show me what you want Steff." He growled, guiding her hand to his cock.

She pressed her lips to his while stroking him with a slight squeeze at his base, just to tease him and make his shaft pulse in her grip.

"I want this, I want tonight, I want you."

"I can give you now, don't know about the night or anything after, but I sure as hell can give you now."

She nodded and he slid first one finger and then a second between her lips stretching her as he stroked her channel that was soaking with arousal. When he pinned her shoulder to the bed with one hand and raised her leg towards her stomach with the other Steff couldn't help but give a shiver of anticipation.

"You alright there, girl?" He asked, his voice rough and strained.

"More than alright, Irish." She said, arching against him.

Rolling her hips against his hand she could feel the tip of his finger nearly touching her g-spot, teasing her with its proximity while denying her the satisfaction she craved. It was a divine torture, and if she could judge by the grin on his face, Mic knew exactly what he was doing. He was enjoying taking her to the edge almost as much as she was enjoying the ride.

She refused give the satisfaction of crying out as the first orgasmic wave crashed over her, and the second. When he leaned down to take her nipple in his again , dragging his teeth over the tight bud, Steff couldn't help but moan his name deliriously.

"Mic, oh god…yes."

"Don't call on the big man yet, hun." He pressed his thumb against her clit and plundered her mouth with a forceful kiss that bordered on a passion she didn't expect.

"I'm just getting started." He growled in her ear as her eyelids fluttered and her body bucked against his hand.

When he flicked the nipple that he had just had in his mouth with his fingers she gasped and then bit her lip. It would take more than that to get the noise from her that she could see he wanted. More was exactly what she needed too.

She let her hands drag over his shoulders as his lips moved down and across her chest. He really was sexy in that dark, dangerous, charming way that melted resolve anywhere he went, including between her legs where his fingers were stroking once again. He worked her body expertly until she gripped his forearm so hard that he switched his attention to her face where she was biting her lip to keep from screaming his name. At this point if she did that it was likely to be loud enough to be heard over the music downstairs and bring at least one curious enforcer to check. She could only hope that it wasn't Whiskey or Satan himself, Mic would likely find himself on the wrong end of their tempers, probably their fists and maybe their boots.

"You gonna tap out sweetheart?" He said, smirking before pressing a kiss to her bellybutton. "Or can you take a little bit more?"

She was trying to find the words to tell him that she wanted everything he had to give her when he stood up and shucked off his pants. When he got back down on the bed

Steff could feel his erection pressing against her thigh while his hand grazed up and down her ribcage.

"No shame in tapping out sweetheart. I'll tell 'em we went all out, and you'll get your bragging rights, or whatever it is you're looking for tonight." Mic murmured softly, surprising Steff with not only his tenderness but his understanding of the need she had to be seen as more than a little sister or child to the men around her.

"I'm not tapping out, Irish. Just letting you know that I'm ready for the main event." She said with a smile, reaching to stroke his length invitingly. "You are what I'm looking for tonight. Let's do this."

She pulled him down to kiss her lips while lifting her hips to meet his body. The thickness of his shaft nudged at her folds, nearly slipping inside her until Mic paused. He brushed a strand of hair from her face and dragged his tongue up her neck.

"You sure about this sweetheart? You have nothing to prove Steff."

"I'm sure Mic." Steff said with a nod, arching against him. "Stop messing around and fuck me."

She shivered when he grinned and pressed into her, with a deviously slow pace. The thickness of his shaft was more than the last man she had been with and the sensation of stretching was incredible. Her body responded to his invasion, to his touch, like a cat that was starved for contact. When he propped himself above her with one hand and began to massage her breast with the other, Steff could have purred like a kitten. It felt so good.

The enthusiasm of other men in the lifestyle was always appreciated and enjoyed. Most of them were one extreme or the other. The younger men were usually rough, rowdy, and positively kinky, and the older men, the ones in their fifties and higher, could be lazy and downright lecherous. It was that magical group, those in their thirties and forties, that had the skills, the passion and, when the time was right, the tenderness of a true Casanova. This was, undoubtedly, the group where Mic was a senior member.

The man knew how to move his body to create a sensual friction that drove her body wild, how to use her in ways that made her feel like she was flying. His mouth, hands and cock were an erotic trifecta of tenderness, pain, and pleasure so intense that it overloaded her every nerve.

Her hand fisted the cheap cotton sheets and Steff arched her back so that her breasts rubbed against his fine, coarse, hair across his chest. Instead of giving her relief, the rubbing made her body tense even more. Everything was pulling tight and the words that Mic was whispering in her ears, whenever he wasn't devouring her body, were taking over even her thoughts. Everything was about the physical sensation, the need to shatter into a million pieces and scream.

"Come on girl. Just give in. You know you want to." He growled, surging deep into her pussy.

"Oh, not yet. God, not yet." Steff whimpered, turning her head to nip at his wrist that was beside her head.

He was balls deep inside her. Every thrust moved her just a little more down the bed and a little bit closer to an orgasm that was likely to bring the roof down on all their heads. She wanted to scream. To feel every nerve ending explode into ecstasy and forget every thought in her head except for him, and the moment of release.

"I've got you girl." Mic grinned and slid both hands behind her back to guide her up so that she was straddling his lap. "Show me what you've got."

Bracing her hands on his shoulder Steff began to ride Mic hard with a pace that was near to frantic. He put one hand on her back and used the other to cup her breast and take it in his mouth.

"Atta girl. Ride that cock." He growled against her chest.

"Oh god, Mic." She cried when, at last, his shaft hit the sweet spot deep inside her that sent her screaming over the edge into bliss.

She barely registered it when her back touched the mattress again, Mic was ramming home in hard, fast strokes that kept her orgasm going in wave after glorious wave and she was screaming his name at each one. Finally, with a long, shuddering stroke, he poured himself into her with a roar of completion.

"Fuck, Steff. You are amazing. The best kept secret in this whole damn club is right here in my arms. I never thought you were that wild." He said, crashing onto the bed beside her. "Never thought I would get a chance to find out either."

"Not many others ever took the chance." She purred in response, laying her head on his chest while he wrapped his arms around her.

"Because most of the members are not so fucking stupid." The voice of Whiskey cut in from the doorway. "Get dressed and get downstairs Steff. Now. Mic, you, and I are going to have a little talk before I drive you home. Move it before I lose my temper."

<u>4</u>

Steff couldn't decide if she was furious or mortified.

Of all the people to catch her in the act it had to be Whiskey. He didn't even have the decency to leave the room while she got dressed. He simply stood and watched with his arms crossed over his chest and a frown so deep it could rival the Grand Canyon.

"Are you going to stare at me this whole time Whiskey? Or can't a lady expect a touch of privacy when she needs to get dressed?" She snapped at him, earning a raised eyebrow from Mic. If he thought that the private enforcer of the club president scared her, even a little bit, then he didn't know her much at all.

"If you were a lady I would not be need to be staring because this wouldn't have happened and it sure as hell wouldn't have happened with him." He jerked a thumb towards Mic.

"And what do you bloody well suggest is wrong with the lady choosing to be with me?" Mic growled, the deliberate emphasis on the word lady telling them both what he thought of Whiskey's insult. "None of you idiots can see what she's worth. You can't really blame a man who can see gem for wanting a chance to touch it, even if he knows he can't keep it."

"You calling me a gem Mic?" Steff asked with a smile, stepping into her shoes with her dress done up. Being fully dressed gave her back her confidence and she wasn't going to accept attitude from Whiskey or any of the other members.

She was certainly allowed to do what she liked with whoever she wanted to.

"It doesn't matter what he's calling you." Whiskey said, opening the door to the hall. "He doesn't have the right, because of who you are."

"Ox will not object and I don't give a damn who my brothers are when they're at home. I am not there, and they don't own me." Steff said as the enforcer half dragged her out of the room.

"I am not talking about your brothers or your boyfriend Steffany. There are others more actively interested in your wellbeing than that lot." Whiskey said, angling his body between her and Mic as they made their way down the stairs.

"No one cares what I do or who I do or don't do Whiskey. I don't know why you've got yourself all wound up about it." The man was infuriating. If he wasn't that rough kind of gorgeous that sent hearts spinning with a grin and a flash of those baby blues she might be able to write him off as a thug of Wrath's, nothing more. She knew though, that he had a warm heart under all that ice and if he was taking an interest in her activities it might be for a reason she didn't know yet.

"I said that I would keep an eye on you and so I will. That includes not letting you get in bed with the mob. Literally." He said, looking over his shoulder at Mic.

"Hey. I'm not going hurt her." The Irishman said with an offended frown. "I like the girl and she likes me back. So calm yourself."

"You shut up and get downstairs. I'll deal with you in a few minutes." He held Steff against the wall with one strong hand just below her neck and jerked his head for the other man to pass them and head downstairs.

"He hurts you, just scream and I'll risk it." Mic said, glaring at Whiskey but heading where he was told.

After a few minutes of silence between them, while waiting for privacy Whiskey released his hand and turned the full force of his icy blue eyes on Steff.

"You listen to me and you listen well, little girl."

"I'm not so little…" She started before he held up a single finger.

"You may not be a member, you may not have a patch, but you're in the lifestyle for sure. You had better act like it when you're not at home." He growled deeply, his finger still in her face. "You are fucking lucky that the brotherhood of your brothers is here to keep you safe. You have no idea the kind of danger you could be in if we weren't."

"Do you think I'm so stupid as to get myself entangled in the mess of things that I'm not supposed to know happen? I'm not one of those patch-bunnies or porn star wannabes you all keep on hand for when you're bored. I am…"

He clamped a hand firmly over her mouth and pressed her back against the wall again. His whole body aligned with hers in a way that let her feel every steel cut inch of him. She could feel his pulse thundering under her palm when she put her hand to his chest, thinking to push him off of her.

His forehead pressed against her and Steff found herself lost for a moment in the blue eyes that had seemed so cold a minute ago but were blazing hot with frustration and anger.

"You are careless because you are protected more than you've ever known. I have told him more times than I can count that's a stupid idea to coddle you like this. It's made you think you're invincible."

"You mean invisible." Steff said sulkily. "No one sees me Whiskey. I am right here, always right here and no one sees me. Ox is the only one who has and now Mic, because he's not one of you. None of you have any concept of the fact that, no matter who my brothers are, I am still a woman. I am flesh and blood and feelings and desires. I am not an angel, of any kind. Why can't you all see that?"

"Oh, so you think we don't see you? You think every member, striker and hang around doesn't look at you like a wild dog looks at a rabbit in a cage." Whiskey growled. His palms planted on the wall to either side of her head kept her boxed in against the wall. "I don't know a man in this house or the one in Nashville that wouldn't take you to bed, or the wall or over the damned pool table if we were allowed to. You, for all of us, are off limits. I have no idea how Ox go the permission to even try let alone hasn't been shot for succeeding."

He straightened and looked her in the eyes as he cupped her chin. Steff trembled just a little, his touch was firm, and his eyes were blazing, but he was right. She was safer than she had ever considered, not because she was cared for, but because someone else had taken away the choice.

"Who the hell said you, or anyone else for that matter, can't have me? Who said you can't want me? Date me? Fuck me? Marry me?" She cried, shoving him away. "Who says I'm not allowed to be loved?"

"The one person who loves you more than any of us ever could." Whiskey said flatly. "Your father."

"My father?" Steff blinked, and her breath caught in her chest. "My father died when Colt and I were babies. Mom told us there was a shoot out in Memphis and Dad got hit shielding Kodiak and Viper. He's dead."

"That shootout happened, I was there too, but your father didn't die. He's got a few more scars than he had before that day, but Steff, your dad is alive, and he loves you enough to stay away. To step away." Whiskey said

"Step away? You think him leaving, if that is what happened, is because he loves me? Loves my brothers? What about my mother who has had to raise us alone?" She snapped, shock and frustration combining into anger at the man who didn't deserve it, and she knew it.

Her mom, Anne, struggled to raise the five of them alone. Even with the help of the club members, who always made sure that birthdays and holidays were amazing, her mom struggled just to keep them all out of jail as kids. Kodiak made it to sixteen before he was arrested, Loch was nineteen, Viper was eighteen and right next to Loch in the cell. She and Colt still hadn't ever seen the inside of a cell. Which mom was grateful for, but it didn't make her hardships any less.

She had watched her mom suffer and struggle and pass up all kinds of opportunities to make the sacrifices needed to give her kids every chance in the world to thrive outside the world of the club. Unfortunately for her, the influence of men like Wrath, who had always been around, like an Uncle, was stronger than she realized. All four boys wore a three-piece patch on their back and a diamond on their left side. Steff would have joined up too, but it was an all male kind of thing. She was as involved as she could be, and her mother hated it.

"Don't get caught up in that world, Steffany." She would say. "You don't want to end up like me with your heart riding around on the seat of a bike, waiting for a call that there was an accident on the highway, or worse, a shooting that took him away without a goodbye. Like your father."

"Why the hell should I respect a man that abandoned me, my family, for my entire life?" She asked him. "Do my brothers know that he's alive? Have they been lying to me too?"

"I don't have the answers you want Steff. I'm sorry." Whiskey said, stepping further back so that she could move down the hall. "I have my orders and all the members downstairs have theirs. I will be taking Mic back to the city and, for your sake, I won't put him in the hospital. He won't be talking to you again. I won't tell anyone what happened, so he should be safe, but he won't be seeing you again."

"You know, since he decided to abandon me and my brothers, I don't think I give a damn about what a man I've never known wants me to do. I'm going to do what and who I want, when I want to and to hell with the feelings of a ghost."

Steff didn't wait for him to answer but stomped down the hall and stairs, passing Satan making out with a girl on the landing. When she made it to the main floor she started to scan the room looking for Brenna. Whiskey came thundering down behind her but didn't touch her or try to stop her.

"Of course, she would pick now, in this place, to disappear with some guy right when I need to get the hell outa here." She muttered looking around the room again.

Mic was at the bar with a drink in his hand, chatting with one of the Boston Duke members. He didn't appear to be roughed up, yet. Steff could only hope and pray that Whiskey would keep his word not to hospitalize him. The older man had never given her a reason not to trust him in all the years she had known him, so she would just have to trust him in this as well.

That didn't mean that she was going to go back on what she said. She was done letting a man she didn't know, didn't even know the real name of, dictate how she was going to live her life. If what she wanted didn't break any of the rules that she and Ox agreed to and if it felt good, she was going to do it whatever, or whoever, it was. The resolve of some of the members might be harder than stone, but others were more malleable. She would start with those ones tonight and then make other, better, decisions tomorrow after she talked to Ox.

Maybe she could convince him to come for a visit to make her feel better about finding out that her dad, her father, that she thought had died to keep her two oldest brothers safe was a bastard. A lousy, family destroying, walkaway-joe, bastard that pretended that he loved his family too much to be a part of it.

Who did that?

A jackass that didn't have what it took to be a real father, let alone a real, big time member of this club. No wonder he'd flaked. She wondered who he had been that his orders were still obeyed since he wasn't the club president, that was Wrath. So, who was her dad?

She walked around the room, smiling, and winking at a few of the younger, less resolved, members. None of them were going to have the information she was after, though they would definitely be physically satisfying. Steff needed to find one of the older guys. Maybe Wrath?

Where was he?

Surely he hadn't left so early in the night? This was a big party and would probably last all weekend.

"Hey man, have you seen the girl I came here with?" She asked the bartender. "And Wrath? I have something I need to talk to him about."

"The girl is upstairs with Satan. They'll be a while if you get me. Wrath is dealing with…business. I doubt you'll talk to him tonight. Sorry kid."

"Satan? And Brenna? My friend, Brenna?"

Steff couldn't believe it. She had told the man to stay away from her. Of all the people she knew in Boston, Brenna was the one who knew how she felt about these guys, Satan especially.

"Fine. I guess I'll just have some fun while I wait to drive her ass home." She said. "Pour me a few shots? If they're going to take a while, then I have time to get drunk. I'll get drunk and still have the time to sober before going home, alone, again."

She slammed back a shot of bourbon.

"Keep 'em coming please." She said, taking the second one, turning the face the room and flashing a smile at the pool table full of men looking at her. "It's a party after all."

<u>5</u>

It definitely was a party and Steff were going to make sure that she didn't remember any more of it than she had to. The music got louder with every shot she took, and it didn't take long until she was dancing around the room, carefree and completely reveling in the attention she was getting. The members were staring, a few were whispering to each other and casting glances towards her.

How many of them wanted her, right now, despite the order? How many of them, who didn't know about Ox, were wanting to take her upstairs and see if what she would let them do? She could see the lust in their eyes, and from the way they sat she could see it in their pants. It was a frustrating shame that, no matter what she did, not a man here would take the chance.

Once again she would wake up alone.

She had hoped, with a few of the mobsters here that she might have had the pleasure of waking up with strong arms wrapped around her.

Mic was still at the bar with Whiskey, both of them were watching her every move. One pair of eyes was bright blue and filled with concern and the other was ice cold and calculating. Whiskey was not done making his point and every inch of his body said that she wasn't going enjoy it. Despite his words upstairs and the reaction of his body against hers it wasn't likely that the enforcer, in his crisp suit that set him so far apart from the other men in the room, would give her the kind of lesson she wished that he would.

Steff knew that Whiskey was that her relationship with Ox was open. He knew that she knew it too. He still hadn't kissed her though. So, either he was full of shit about hot the guys felt about her or he was truly terrified of whoever had told them all to stay away from her.

Why hadn't he kissed her? And why was he sitting next to Mic?

Both of them were staring at her while she moved. It was easy to tell that both of them were thinking about a vastly different kind of dancing. Steff had to test the resolve of the Duke and the restraint of the mobster. Could they manage to keep their hands to themselves?

"You got something you need to say to me, Whiskey?" She said, stepping up to him and sliding her hands up his thighs. "Anything you want there, buddy? Anything at all?"

She was practically purring, leaning forward so that he couldn't help but stare down the front of her dress. She wondered if he even realized that he had licked his lips?

"Girl, you are about five minutes away from deserving a spanking and I'm about six minutes away from delivering it."

She threw back her head and laughed.

"You gonna balls up and do it yourself or will you send me to my Daddy?"

Whiskey's indulgent smile turned to a frown and Mic intervened.

"Steff? Maybe you should take it easy. I think you've pushed him far enough tonight."

The mobster put his hand on her shoulder but before she could say anything to him about it, Whiskey was on his feet.

He moved so fast that Steff fell backwards, landing on her backside.

"I told you not to touch her ever again, you stupid little shit." He snapped. Driving his fist across Mic's jaw.

Mic fell backwards off the stool but got back up and returned the blow, causing other members to grab hold of both men and start to wrestle them towards the door. Steff got to her feet and tried to follow the rabble. She was trying to get Whiskey's attention, trying to get the attention of any of them so that she could put a stop to the violence. There was no need for it. He had only put his hand on her shoulder.

"Hold on there girlie." A voice she didn't know whispered in her ear as arms wrapped around her waist and pulled her backwards. "That's not the place for you. Someone else wants to see you tonight."

No one noticed that she wasn't with them.

No one heard her call for help.

Even Whiskey was too focused on pummeling Mic to look back to see her.

One of the hands from her waist slid, snake-like, up her torso squeezing her breast before clamping over her mouth to cover her scream.

"Oh yes, the boss is going to enjoy getting his hands on you, almost as much as he's going to enjoy getting his cock in you." The voice that she still didn't recognize whispered in her ear before he bit the lobe hard.

When she screamed again and bit down on his hand he spun her around and the last thing she knew was his hand smashing across her face hard enough to knock her into the wall. Then it all went black.

She woke up in the back seat of a truck, her hands zip-tied together just like the cops had done to Colt once in high school. Her head was on someone's lap and there was a hand down the top of her dress, fondling her breast with a casual, almost slack grip. It was like he had been doing it for a while and was bored or something.

"Stop touching me." She said, trying to sit up.

The hand moved from her breast to her head, holding her in place.

"I don't think I will. Unless you're gonna roll over and me another kind of pleasing, I'll keep my hand just where I want it."

He was too calm, too smug. This wasn't random and these couldn't be members of the club or the mafia. They wouldn't do this.

None of them would ever do this.

She wanted to scream, to fight, but there was no point while they were moving. Everything Kodiak and Viper had told her when she was younger was running through her head. Stay calm and look for a chance to escape. She wiggled her feet, trying to get her heels to fall off so that she would be able to run.

A hand from the front seat reached over and pulled the bottom of her dress up before slapping her ass hard. When she yelped there was a twitch in the pants her face was pressed against and his hand tightened.

"Sounds like we got a live one here, boys." He laughed and slapped her bare skin again. It was harder than the man in the front and he left his hand resting on her ass. His fingers tracing the welt she could feel rising. "I'm going enjoy my turn with this one more than the rest. Who would have thought Razor's little bitch would be so tasty?"

"How tasty is that cunt?" The driver called, reaching over the seat to put his hand on Steff's hip.

The guy holding her head in his lap must be sitting behind the driver, which meant when they stopped for gas she could throw the other nozzles and hoses at him and the man holding her head so she could run. That might let her get into the gas station or at least into the sight of the attendant and a camera. God, she shuddered to think what they had planned for her if they got her where they wanted. They obviously knew who she was or thought they did. She had no idea who Razor was, she'd never heard the name before. It must be who her father is, or was, when he was a member.

"I'm not who you think I am. You should let me go. I haven't seen your faces. I can't tell anyone who you are." She tried pleading. It might work. She didn't recognize their voices, so she didn't know them well enough to ID them to anyone, even Ox and her brothers.

"You are exactly who we think you are, Princess. Razor's daughter, Wrath's niece, and stepdaughter. Twisted fucking sickos that your parents are. Kodiak is your brother, so is Viper and Loch, who just got shot today so he WAS your brother. Colt is the next one to go down."

Loch couldn't be dead. Not her smartass big brother. He was too mean to die and if someone had hurt him then they wouldn't live long. If the bastards meant to kill the whole family then she was as good as dead too if she didn't get away. They would torture her, rape her and gods knew what else before they did it, but they meant to kill her. The man by her feet was still talking about her family and as he did he forced her legs apart, slapping her thighs when she tried to close them.

"Then there's our little brood mare here." He said slapping his hand down hard on her mound before circling his thumb around her clit. "I wonder how long it'll take to get her bred after the boss makes his point? The look on ol' Razor's face, right before we put a bullet through it, will almost be better than tonight will be. When we show him the video of his baby girl taking every cock in the platoon and every shot the boss takes in this little pussy right before we let him know that the little heifer is heavy with Daggers baby his face is gonna crumble and then the asshole is going to die knowing that we got the only one of his kids left living breeding for our side."

"You dirty sons of bitches." Steff growled, hating that her body responded to what he was trying to do. "I won't do it. Hell no. Get off me."

"Sassy little thing, isn't she?" The man with his hands between her legs said, right before he rammed his fingers into her.

She screamed in protest, but the sound was muffled when her face was pressed against the erection now tenting the pants of the man holding her head tight. They all laughed while she fought against them both. They weren't even trying to hurt her. The bastard was actually trying to get her off and, damn him to hell, he might succeed. She hated them, all of them, and if she lived through this there would not be one day that she would not be working towards their demise. That thought was what she fought to hold on to when her head was pulled back just far enough that the dick her face had been pressed against could be pulled out of his pants and forced between her lips.

"You bite that and I'm gonna knock out your teeth and use your bloody mouth as lube for your ass. You understand me? Now be a good girl and you'll get a tasty treat for supper." He said, pulling her hair into a ponytail to use as a handle and force her head to move up and down on his bristly cock.

He tasted like sweat and obviously hadn't shaved recently because she could feel the stubble at his base rubbing the inside of her lip until she tasted her own blood.

Steff was dimly aware of a flash going off and assumed that the man in the front that wasn't driving had just taken a photo of what was happening to her. It was hard to tell what was going on, she was trying not to gag or cry around the disgusting piece of flesh in her mouth, at the same time she was fighting her body's reaction to the fingers that were bringing her closer to an orgasm that she didn't want to have.

"Just look at her." One of the voices from the front seat said. "The little wench likes it. Make her cum Ricky. I wanna taste that sweetness."

The man, Ricky, shifted his fingers and, as much as she hated herself for it, Steff couldn't help the wave of release that came with the touch against her g-spot. She screamed around the cock that was starting to twitch in her mouth, hoping that she might be spared swallowing his cum, and her eyes flashed open when she felt the stab of a needle in her hip.

"There. Keep her high on that while she cums and by the time Dagger puts a dick in that pussy she'll be jonesing for the high. Won't you kitten?" The voice from the front said as she slipped into a state of oblivion.

What the hell was in that needle?

<u>**6**</u>

Most of the drive was a blur.

They kept her high, on the edge of arousal and orgasm the whole time but Steff knew that it had to be at least two days. Each of the men had changed their seat positions twice that she could remember, rotating between driving, sleeping in the front seat or occupying one of the spaces in the back seat and tormenting her any way that they could without actually fucking her.

She had been fingered, eaten out, had her ass eaten before they'd plugged her. She could vaguely remember them laughing when she whimpered as Seth, the man who had originally held her head, pushed the piece between her cheeks. John had been the driver when she had first been brought to the truck, his favorite thing was to cum on her face after forcing her to suck him hard. Abe was the man with the needle, he liked pain, so everything he did to her involved slapping, pinches, and spanking. He scared her the most of all four of them.

She had expected threats and violence, maybe being roughed around a little bit when they'd taken her. Sexual torment and the degradation of being forced to cum for them, repeatedly, was unexpected and was more than she knew how to handle. Whatever was in the needle was keeping her just on the edge of consciousness. She could hear them, feel them, but she couldn't fight them. She couldn't fight the waves of physical pleasure they were forcing on her body and she hated herself for it. No matter what she thought of, it didn't help.

They had watched her for every second, even in the bathroom she had one of them with her. Her feet hurt from walking on hot concrete and gravel at the roadside stops. The drug kept her in a state that was like being drunk but semi euphoric as well. She had never done this, whatever it was, and she could already feel how dangerous it was.

She hated them and what they were doing to her, even though the injections made it physically pleasurable. She could already, after two days of constant use, feel her body craving it when the doses started to wear off. If she survived this, if she escaped or Ox and her brothers were able to rescue her, the detox from this drug was going to be a new kind of torture.

"Hey. We're getting close to the bunker. Make sure she's awake and dressed. Dag is going to want her ready for him."

"Sit up, pussy cat." Ricky said, tugging her upright while talking to her as if she had a choice. "Take a drink and get ready for the boss. He's going to be happy to see your pretty little face."

Steff sucked back the cool water, grateful that it was cold and fresh, unlike her right now. She also noticed that the men were treating differently now that they were arriving at the location. There was no more probing fingers or teasing, they were all business now. Though it was good to know that they were scared of Dagger, it also meant that she should be scared of him too.

Her skin was pinpricked and itching. She was starting to fidget. It had been a few hours since they had injected her and she was starting to notice, to think about it. She had to get away before she needed it more than she wanted it. She knew that this could be her chance to run and she should take it, but could she do it? The only thing she'd had eaten since they had grabbed her was a chocolate bar and some beef jerky. If she had the strength to run she would have to make it count.

"Where am I? Where is this place?" Steff asked, looking around, trying to get an idea of what might be a way of escape or what direction she should try to run in.

"This, kitten, is the bunker." Ricky said, opening the door and helping her out of the truck.

The truck had parked next to a grey metal sided building with a dingy door that once was blue but had faded and peeled from neglect. Looking around Steff couldn't see a sign of any other buildings and she couldn't hear the traffic of a highway. Her heart sank, it was likely that they were too far off the main road for her to get where anyone could see her, let alone help her. She had to try though. As soon as Ricky let go of her she would run, screaming, just in case there was anyone outside that might hear her. Abe, Seth, and John got out of the truck as well and stood, stretching their legs while they shared a grin and lit their smokes. Steff was playing along, stretching as well as rolling her shoulders, waiting for just the right moment.

Stepping out of her shoes she was grateful that it was packed dirt and not loose gravel under her feet. She might be able to run further than she thought if it was like this. Bending at the waist to touch her toes Steff glanced under the truck to see that the driveway was packed dirt with a patch of grass down the middle. That would be great to run on, and it probably led to a highway.

"Mm, get used to that position, kitten." Abe said, stepping up behind her and gripping her hips. "I'm gonna be pounding that ass for hours tonight."

"Like hell you are." Steff snapped back, grabbing both shoes and smashing one across Abe's face, the heel drawing blood before she threw one at Ricky and one at John. She shoved Seth against the truck and took off running down the road.

Once she cleared the yard that they had pulled into Steff started to call for help, screaming louder as she got further away. She could hear the men yelling and swearing, trying to organize themselves enough to chase her down. She had to keep going, her lungs were on fire and her feet hurt but she was almost there.

She could see the road, there wasn't much traffic on it, which told her that they weren't anywhere near a state capitol. She could, faintly, hear the buzz of a bike though. There was a fifty percent chance of the rider being a member of a club. That meant she would be safe. No member of any club was going ignore a woman on the side of the road, especially one that had obviously been roughed up. She had to get to the road before he passed the driveway. She absolutely had to get his attention and get away from this place and these monsters.

"Come on, be wearing a cut." She muttered once she got to the highway.

Sprinting towards the oncoming bike she felt a piece of glass cut her foot but didn't care. She had to get him to stop because she knew that she couldn't bear getting back into that truck. Everything in her body hurt and she was seeing spots, but this was the only chance she was going to get.

"Hey there honey." The rider slowed down and pulled onto the shoulder. "You alright? Looks like you've found yourself a bit of trouble."

He was wearing a vest but there were no patches on it. It was a clean cut. He wasn't a member of a club, but he was likely more than the average rider. He was safer than the alternative. He had to be.

"You could say that. Can you get me off this road?" She pointed back over her shoulder. "That truck right there is filled with the trouble that I'm trying to get away from. Please?"

She hated to beg but if he refused she had to keep running.

He pulled down his sunglasses to take a closer look at her, all the way down to her bare feet. His eyes were warm and clear. He probably had a few questions about what a girl in a filthy party dress was doing out in the middle of the countryside, but he didn't ask them. He simply looked towards the truck where Abe and Seth were standing in the truck bed watching, then looked back at her.

"Get on." He nodded towards the seat behind him. "We'll get this sorted out."

She climbed on behind him and wrapped her arms around his chest.

"Thanks. Thanks so much. I'm Steff. I'm from Nashville and been going to school in Boston. Where am I?" She asked, tucked in behind him as he started the bike up again.

"You're in Colorado and you can call me Banner."

"Like the sign?" She asked with a faint smile. Being rescued was enough of a relief to give her a bit of a smile.

"Like the fictional scientist. It's a reminder to keep my temper. My little sister called me that since we were kids." He said over his shoulder.

"That's kinda funny. Wait. No. This isn't the way." She realized that he had turned down the drive she had just escaped from.

"Sure it is. I own this place. Why? What's the matter?" He pulled the bike into the garage and turned around to look at her. "We can call whoever you need and get this straightened out."

"We'll take this little bitch from here Banner." John said, grabbing Steff by this hair, making her scream and twist in his grip.

"Don't let them. Please. Please!" She begged Banner when Abe grabbed her at the knees and pinched.

"That's for the cut on my face, bitch, and I'm not done with you yet." He growled in her ear.

"What the hell man? What're you doing to her. She needs help, to get home or at least back to school." Banner got off the bike and started walking towards them. "I told her she could call her brothers."

"She's not calling anyone, and neither are you." A voice that Steff knew, and hated, called from the doorway. Machete.

"She is exactly why we're here and you're going to shut your mouth about it. To the bunker, now, all of you." Machete said, walking up to Steff with a terrifying grin on his face. "The boss is waiting."

She was about to scream, again, when he leaned forward and kissed her on the mouth. The stubble from his unshaven face rubbed her skin raw and his tongue was licking her lower lip and chin. He tasted like cheap gin and stale cigarettes. It made Steff want to puke.

Banner stepped in and pulled Machete back with a growl.

"Hey man, she's just a kid. Get off her."

Steff could see by the look on his face that he had no idea what the others had planned. He wasn't in on this.

"Banner, you gotta help me. Call my brothers. In Nashville. The Dukes of Hell clubhouse, call them, ask for Colt, or Loch. Please! They'll send Ox."

They were carrying her towards the bunker, but she still had eyes on Banner and Machete. Her heart froze when the old man pulled out a gun to point at the biker.

"You signed on to help us with this and you're going to. You even think of calling that house and I'll put one between your eyes."

"I didn't sign on to kidnap college kids and I sure as hell didn't sign on for rape." He said, pointing towards Steff. "Just let her go. What beef could you have with a kid her age man?"

"Her old man and his brother are going to suffer for what they did to me and mine. She's the little princess of that club and she's how we make them pay."

Machete gripped Banner by the collar and dragged him towards the bunker where Steff was twisting and struggling, trying to keep from getting taken inside.

"It's not right. She's just a kid." Banner said, trying to shrug off Machete's grip. "I'm not going to hurt her."

"You're going to do what you're told and that means that you're going to face the same consequences as the rest of us if this goes south. You're all in too and we're going to make sure of that tonight." Ricky said with a grin. "You can enjoy it or not, but you're a part of this."

"I'm not fucking touching her. Hell no." Banner said, looking Steff in the eye. "I'm not that kind of guy."

The four men from the truck laughed and Machete lowered his gun as a door opened on the other side of the bunker.

"That's alright, Banner, we're willing to train you to be our kind of guy." Dagger said, crossing the floor and running his hand down Steff's leg. "Put her down boys. There's nowhere for her to run now."

John and Abe set Steff down, John's knife cutting the strap of her dress as her feet touched the ground. She didn't care what they said, or that all of them, except Banner, were laughing as she tried the entrance. Even throwing herself against it didn't budge the metal door. After the third try she had to stop, it hurt too much, and she was feeling dizzy. Looking at the way Dagger and Machete were undressing her with their eyes made her nauseous in a way that had nothing to do with the drug in her system.

"It's not going to move for you, girl. You're just going to hurt yourself if you keep trying." Dagger said, walking towards her. He snapped his fingers, commanding Seth, and Ricky to fall into step behind him. "There's nothing you can do except for surrender. It will be a lot more fun for you if you do."

"Screw you Dagger. Never gonna happen. I will fight you every second until I'm out of here." Steff spat the words at him.

"I think our guest has forgotten just how good it can feel to comply with what we want." Dagger said with a smirk that chilled Steff's blood. "You boys got those needles ready? I'd hate for her to start getting itchy and twitchy, jonesing for it like streetwalking junkie.”

He leaned in close to Steff, running his fingers up her arms while she shivered, fighting the exact symptoms he just described.

“That’s not going to be me. Not me.” She shook her head and squeezed her eyes shut while the old man started to kiss her neck while groping her breast. “Not me.”

She had to separate herself from this, not let this define her. She couldn’t stop them, but she could stop herself from giving them the fearful response they obviously wanted from her.

“Oh yes, you.” He growled, biting her neck, and yanking her dress up over her hips and fumbling with his belt.

“No!” Steff tried to fight him, struggling until he put a hand on her throat. She could feel his erection pressing against her stomach and remembered Loch telling her how, more than anyone else he knew, Dagger got off on a woman’s fear of him.

“Holy fuck.” Steff heard Banner yell, his boots stomping across the floor. “I’m not going to let you do this. She’s just a damn kid. Get the hell off her.”

Steff opened her eyes, choking on the grip. Her eyes locked to Banner’s just before John pulled a pistol and pointed it at the centre of the leather clad chest. Abe and Ricky grabbed hold of his arms and John grinned.

“Don’t worry. You’ll be sticking it in her soon enough buddy. No choice in that.”

"Like hell I will. You sick fuck." He replied, only to be met with the fist of Ricky knocking him across the head.

She watched the only man that could save her fall to his knees, taking a blow to the head from each of the men holding his arms behind his back. With the gun in play and both Dagger and Machete in the room, if Banner wasn't careful he was going to end up dead. That would be the end of her too. Right now, he was her only hope.

"Pull his head up." Machete said, cracking a beer. "Make him watch. Keep those eyes open boy or I'll have her riding your cock. Makes you just as guilty as us in the eyes of those brothers of hers."

Steff couldn't believe the nightmare that she was living but when Ricky pulled Banner's head up and Dagger tightened his grip on her throat it was impossible to ignore. This was happening and unless someone figured out what happened in Boston, or Banner kept to his conscience as well as managed to escape or get out of this building alone and alive, Dagger's plan was going to succeed. A point that was made even clearer when she felt the wetness at the tip of his bare cock wipe against her stomach, just above her belly button.

"No, no, no. Please no." She begged, squeezing her eyes shut and tightening her hands into fists, as if that could stop him.

Dagger laid her back across the metal top of a freezer and pulled her hips right to the edge. When Steff started to kick and squirm he slapped her hard across the face and gripped her inner thigh tight.

"That's right, kitten, beg for me." He growled just before pressing his thick cock into her core.

The pull and stretch of her body around him hurt but it was the way that it started to feel good that made her want to scream, which she couldn't do. If she let him know that she was afraid it would make him harder, more vicious, and give him exactly what he wanted from her. Steff knew it was the drug and the way they had conditioned her in the truck that made it feel good. She didn't want this, and she never would, but her body wasn't registering this as assault. God damn the man on top of her. With one hand kneading her breast and the other playing with her clit, he was going to make her cum.

It was hopeless, crude, demeaning, disgusting and cruel. If she ever got out of here she would hate him forever and do anything and everything she could to end the man thrusting into her body with shallow, weak motions. She could smell the booze on his breath and feel the shake in his knees. Despite his hatred he still needed false courage and bravado to fuel his convictions that what he was doing, what he was going to let happen, wasn't purely monstrous.

Looking up at the ceiling Steff let the tears of defeat roll down her cheeks. If even her body was betraying her what chance did she have to survive this with anything resembling sanity?

Dagger finished his assault with a grunt and a flick of his tongue up her cheek, lapping up her tears.

"Not bad for a first round. You'll be better next time when you're begging for that needle. Machete, your turn with her." Dagger said, stepping back and taking a beer from the other man.

"Thank you, brother." Machete said, taking a needle from Seth and flipping Steff over to inject the fluid into her ass cheek. "Seems only right that we're the ones breeding this little bitch. Since we should have been her daddies instead of Wrath and Razor."

"What the hell do you mean you two sickos should have been her daddies?" Banner asked from his knees with the pistol still pointing at him. "You're doing this to your own kid? Or stepdaughter? What the fuck is wrong with you?"

"Her mother, Anne, was supposed to be mine." Dagger said, slamming back a can of beer while his eyes stayed locked on Steff, who was being pressed into the cold metal surface.

"Instead, the bitch chose marry Razor, then Wrath, then sleep with Razor again when Wrath cheated on her with Liz and had that arrogant piece of shit son of his. She raised five kids with those two brothers and yet never gave us the time of day. So instead of fucking her, I intend for the two of us to breed fuck her baby girl, their baby girl, as one of the many acts of retribution for kicking us, and our associates out of the Dukes. They said we were criminal, evil, not worthy of the patch. Well…" He paused to grip Steff by the hair and turn her face towards Banner. "If they want to see evil, we're going to give it to them. In ways that they'll never see coming and can't undo no matter how hard they try."

The drug was coursing through her system already, making it hard to think and even harder to speak or cry out as he kicked her legs apart and positioned himself behind her. Even though she knew it was useless, they wouldn't listen even if they understood her, Steff did her best to say no, to make sure that she made it clear that she wasn't willing. No matter what her body did in response to the forced stimulation, she did not want this, didn't like it, and refused to simply accept it.

"Hear that sound boys?" Machete laughed. "Sounds like she's getting in the spirit of things."

Unlike Dagger, Machete wasn't weak or shaking. He was driven, angry and taking all that out on Steff. She could feel his hatred as he pinched and prodded her body. She didn't know him well enough to know what got him hard, what got him off, but he was enough like Dagger that she knew that it couldn't be good. When he wet his thumb and gripped her like a bowling ball she couldn't help but cry out and thrash against him.

"You two are twisted fucks, you know that." Banner said, shaking his head in disgust. "I hope her brothers, whoever they are, take their time killing you."

"Would one of you shut him up. He's messing with my enjoyment of the moment." Machete growled. He put his hand on the back of Steff's neck, pressing her into the metal again with the weight of his body.

Steff closed her eyes when she saw Seth walking towards the others, slipping on a leather glove with metal knuckles that shone in the florescent light. She heard the impact of the blow and the thud as Banner hit the ground. There would be no reprieve now, no voice of reason to dissuade the four men from the truck to stop what was happening, or at least not actively participate in the assault.

"Open up for me baby. I wanna feel every inch of that sloppy wet hole." He grunted, sliding his cock up and down between her ass cheeks.

She could feel him getting harder, hear his breath catching when his balls nestled against her. When he was done trying to impregnate her there was no doubt where he really wanted to fuck her. She whimpered and he laughed.

"That's right, the boys plugged this tight little ass on the ride, and you went wild for it. The video they sent of you begging for more, grinding on Ricky's hand while they pumped it in and out of you."

"You want me to get the plug Chet?" Ricky asked eagerly. Steff could tell by the bulge in his pants that the show, the torture, was getting him hot and hard.

"Nah. I think she's ready for the real thing." He replied, spitting on her entrance, and repositioning himself. "Come hold her down and get a good look at how well that drug works."

<u>8</u>

Ricky gripped Steff by the back of the head, keeping her steady while Machete nudged the head of his cock past her entrance, spitting on her more than once to lube the thick, pulsing length. It felt like he was going to rip her in two as he speared her ass. She could feel his hands, one in the small of her back to press her down, while the other was on her ass cheek, pulling her further open. When he was fully sheathed inside her, pulsing while Steff ached and wept.

When he started to move inside her, getting her blood pumping she finally felt the drug beginning to take effect. It would have been so much easier if he would just hurt her. At least she wouldn't hate herself for feeling pain, but the injections that took away the pain, that made her moan with pleasure like a whore or a porn star, took away her self-respect and gave way too much joy to her captors.

"See boys? If you want to subdue a woman stick your cock up her ass and watch her cum, begging for more."

Steff felt Ricky remove his hands, everyone knew he didn't need to hold her down now. Her ass was bouncing up and down Machete's cock, every thick, veiny inch stimulating her body. Her stupid, betraying body that was proving him right. She propped herself up on her hands, changing the angle of his penetration to stroke even closer to that spot that was going to make her scream.

"Atta girl, Steffy. Show me how bad you want it. Ride that cock, you dirty little slut." Machete chuckled and licked her neck.

"I am dirty, so dirty." Steff mumbled deliriously. "More."

She meant the drug, but he looped an arm around her neck and lifted Steff off the freezer to turn her to face the others.

"The bitch wants more, gents. Who's gonna give it to her?"

"Too bad Banner's out of the game. This would make a great little initiation for him, crossing swords with the boss." John said with a laugh, stepping up to Steff and slipping a finger up her pussy. "So tight in there, I don't think another cock is gonna fit."

When he bent down to lick between her legs Abe jumped to his feet.

"Hey, he might not want to, or be able to join, but if you want own his fucking ass we can make it look like he played along. Seth, you hold the camera. John, you help me move him into place."

"I like how your twisted little mind works, Abe." Dagger said watching the men position Banner over Steff's lap.

She tried to push him off, he didn't deserve what would happen to him if the boys ever saw that but Machete took one of her hands in his and placed the other on the unconscious man's head, holding her hand and his head in place while he pumped into her ass. The camera went off a few times, each flash making him twitch deep inside her.

He got off on being watched, on being the center of attention. That was why there was camera's and studio lights all around the room. He was going to film himself and the others fucking her, raping her, getting her high so that she'd beg them to do unspeakable things to her in exchange for more of the drug that made the pain go away.

"That'll do. Let him drop so I can finish. You boys deserve a turn to play with this little slut while she's still enjoying herself."

Her cries of protest were ignored as Machete bent her back over the freezer, pinned her arms above her head and rode her ass hard and fast until he spilled into her with a groan of deep satisfaction. When his empty, flaccid dick slid out, Steff felt a trickle of fluid follow after him and she cried out in protest, but she wasn't sure if it was the completion of the act or withdrawal of the sensations that she was angry about.

When he stepped away Machete invited Seth and the others to take a turn finishing what they had started in the truck while they'd traveled from Boston.

"Just remember this, boys: I don't care where or how you fuck her. However, if you spill even a drop inside while we're trying to breed her then I'll cut your pecker off and leave you pissing in a bag for the rest of your life." Machete said, cracking open another beer. "And keep her buzzing on those injections. In a few days she'll be hooked and then we'll be able to do the video for her brothers and that boyfriend of hers."

Abe dragged Steff's drugged and dazed Steff over to a dingy mattress on an old bedframe and placed a pair of metal cuffs on a long chair that was threaded around the headboard on her wrists.

"You gonna text it to them?" He asked, standing to undo his belt and jeans.

"Nah, I think it needs to be put in their hands, with proof that we really have her and not some girl done up to look like her." Dagger said, setting up a tripod that was pointing at the bed.

"Jeezus, who gets that suicide mission?" John asked, sitting down, and kicking his feet up.

"Oh, I think our boy Banner gets to do that. Just in case they want to shoot the messenger in a very literal sense. One of you will drive him to Nashville, his bike in the back of your truck, hand him the tape and remind him of our leverage. He'll do exactly what we tell him to do and he'll do it well."

"What leverage do we have with him? I know we're on his land, which should give him leverage." Ricky asked, sitting by Steff's head, and running his fingers through her hair, making it impossible for her to dream herself away from the reality of the man on top of her and the horrors facing her future.

"We have his only sister, not here, but we could have her hear within a day. If he doesn't play it our way then Steff is going to have a new roommate."

"Shit."

They all chuckled.

"That'd do it. We can probably get him to do just about anything now." John said. "You sure you want to waste it on that video?"

Dagger laughed and the sound made Steff shudder, which brought a groan of satisfaction from Abe.

"Banner will drop off the video, they'll blow his brains out for being involved and we'll have Steff and his sister anyway. She inherits the lands, one of us marries her and takes over, the other marries Steff so that when we finish killing off her family and she inherits everything from them, we get that too."

"You're going to marry them?" Ricky asked. "After all this fucking you want them to be the 'little woman' at home with the babies and all that fifties crap?"

"No. We're going to own them, legally. Then once they've each popped out an heir and a spare we're going to make them earn every second they want with those kids on their back, knees, stomach in front of the camera or behind closed doors for cash. We'll be raking in the dough for every cock that they touch. Fucked to death, or until they're too used up and ugly to turn a profit."

"Sounds like a good business plan boss." John said with a grin. "Might find myself a little clubhouse heiress and join you."

"There is no bike club in the world that is going to touch this kind of stuff, so we'll have a good lock on it. I think there's a niece of Razor's in Louisiana. We can get her hooked on this joy juice and take down another chapter, plus that arrogant muscle in a suit's been dating her."

"Whiskey?" Abe asked, getting off the bed and leaving Steff naked and dazed on the mattress, listening but unable to speak. "I'd love the chance to take him down a peg or two."

"Alright." Dagger said gesturing for the other men to join him at the table. "If we're going to take down the Dukes, the whole club, we need a better plan. Make sure that Banner is still out cold and get over here."

Seth checked on the man laying on the floor where they'd dropped him.

"Yeah, the cowboy's still out cold. Let's get this done."

While the six men gathered round the table, drinking and plotting, occasionally looking over towards Steff, she tried not to think about what her life was looking like from this night onwards. She could barely move, between the chains and the drugs, but she could turn her head. When she did she could have sworn that she saw Banner looking at her, then at the table, with something in his hand.

What was he doing?

Steff wished there were a chance that she wouldn't remember this night. That this was going to be something that a therapist could make disappear with some talk sessions and maybe medication. When they started talking about their plans to take down every chapter of the Dukes of Hell that they could find a weakness in, she knew that she had to remember every word of it. If she ever saw Ox and her brothers again, when she saw them again, she was going to need to be able to tell them everything.

The six men were so engrossed in their plans that they didn't notice the red light on Banner's phone as he lay on the floor. She was right, he was recording them. Hopefully, that meant that he had some kind of plan to get them both out of this place and safely to The Court in Nashville.

If he didn't get caught first.

She had to distract them, make sure that their attention was on her and not on him at all. There was only one thing that she could think of to ensure that.

She started to moan, and writhe on the bed, half faking but half truly feeding the need for another round of the stuff that they had injected her with.

"Well now, look who's getting alert." Dagger said with a grin, setting down the knife that had been in his hand. "We can't have that now, can we? Seth, get her booster ready."

He stalked towards the bed. His eyes locked to hers. If she could have run screaming she would have, but that was more than impossible. She had to stay and suffer through whatever he was going to do so that there was a chance that she and Banner would both get out of this place alive.

"John, turn her over. Face down and ass up, looking at the cameral. Ricky, you, and Abe get that spotlight and the camera. I think it's time we make a little home movie." Dagger said, unfastening his belt, drawing it through the loops on his jeans before laying a hard strike across her backside.

When she screamed, he dropped his pants to the floor and motioned for Machete to join him.

"Make sure that you get all of this on film." Dagger said, caressing the rising welt. "I want Razor and Wrath to get a good eye full of us turning their little girl into a cock-hungry whore."

Ricky and Abe chuckled and adjusted the camera and lights while that pair of men set to work to tease and arouse Steff's protesting body. She had thought that they would just smack her around and do what they were going to do. She wasn't prepared for them to work hard to turn her on, making the traces of the drug in her system work against her mind.

"Please. Oh god, please." She moaned, closing her eyes.

She wanted them to stop, to just be allowed to fall asleep. Even though she had started this it wasn't supposed to feel good, she wasn't supposed to want more. When she arched her back to press against the hand between her legs she hated that it felt good.

"Told you that stuff would work for us." Machete said, slapping her in the face with his cock. "Open up kitten. Let's get this show started."

<u>9</u>

She tried to bury her face in the mattress. The only resistance she had left was in small acts like this. It didn't work though. Dagger slapped his hand against the dampness between her legs and wrenched her head to the side so that Machete could pry her mouth open.

"Remember, if you bite down you won't get any of the joy juice." He said, gripping the back of her head.

They took their time, used every trick to bring physical pleasure to a woman that they knew, and they knew a lot. Even though she hated them, and what they were doing, Steff heard herself begging for more. That's when she felt the needle press into her thigh and a few minutes later she blacked out.

When she woke up enough to force her eyes open Steff was laying flat on the bed and her whole body hurt. There were two belts on the bed beside her and she could faintly feel welts rising on her ass and legs. Her jaw hurt, so did her head. There were pull marks on her wrists, the bed had moved from the wall and she could feel liquid dripping between her thighs.

What had happened after the drug kicked in?

She couldn't remember anything after she had begged for more.

The camera was being put away and the bright light had been turned out. Steff was starting to shiver as cold night air crept in while the men moved a few things out the door of the bunker.

"We'll send a copy of that film along to your big brothers and that boyfriend of yours, Kitten. Maybe that'll get dear ol' Daddy's attention." Dagger said, sitting down on the bed to give her a drink of water and pull a scratchy wool blanket over her. "In the meantime, I'm gonna keep you on your back making me happy with those legs wide open."

Steff cringed when he rubbed her stomach and leaned forwards to kiss her forehead.

"You be a good girl and get some sleep. Another big day tomorrow, we've got lots of work to do and you're the center of it all."

Tears rolled down her cheeks as they flicked out each of the lights. Abe checked to make sure that Banner was still unconscious, gave him another hard kick and locked the door behind him as he left.

When the sound of the deadbolt clicked in place and she was alone in the dark there was no need to put on a brave face anymore, no one to see or hear as she broke down into wailing sobs of despair. Steff pulled her knees to her chest and tried to move her shacked wrists enough to hold herself in a ball. She needed to hold herself together so that she could face whatever new horrors those bastards came up with for tomorrow. Somehow she had to find strength to persevere, memories to hold on to, and most importantly, a hope that when it was all done, that Ox would be able to see past what was done to her. Whatever that video might show, the things she remembered and the things that she couldn't, she prayed that Ox would still see her under the shadows of pain and the haze of the drug.

See her, love her and, somehow, forgive her.

It might be too much to ask of him, but she had to hope that it was possible, or she had nothing left to hold on to. The fear of having to face life after this alone was almost as terrifying as facing what was to come.

That thought ripped another ragged sob from her chest that turned into a yelp when a hand touched her shoulder and Banner's voice spoke softly next to her head.

"Hey kid. Don't give up just yet. You're not in this alone now."

"Banner? I thought they knocked you out. Can you get us out of here?"

"I think so. I still have some keys on me. They knocked me around pretty good, but I managed to stay conscious once I woke up from the first time." He sat down on the edge of the bed and opened a fresh bottle of water for each of them. "Take a drink of that. Try to clear your head while I figure out which keys I have and what I can do with them."

Steff sat up as much as she could and took a few long sips from the bottle. It was cool and refreshing so she poured some into her hand washed her face and as much of her body as she could. It wasn't enough but it was a start, maybe just enough that she would be able to sleep.

"Is there anything you can see to eat?" She asked, wrapping the blanket around herself to try and stop the shivering. "Are they still awake? Can you see anything out there?"

It might be too much to hope that all six of them would be so confident in their schemes that they would get drunk and go to sleep without setting a guard or coming back to the bunker to check on her, but she was hoping regardless.

"I don't see anything to eat and I'm sorry, I don't keep stashes of food out here." Banner replied from the back of the building. "On a good note it looks like they're drinking in the kitchen, which benefits us on two levels."

"If they're drunk they'll be sloppy and less likely to bother coming out here to check on things. What else does it do?" Steff asked.

"It means that we can get out of here through the back door, which I have a key for, get on my bike and get out of here." He said with a determination in his voice.

He must have missed the part of the plan where they had his little sister in their sights. If he hadn't then he clearly didn't understand just how vicious these men could be.

"Not us, just you Banner." She said to him when he came back to the bed with a saw in his hands. "That'll take too long to get me free and…"

"No ands or buts kiddo. I gotta get you out of here too. There is no way that I'm leaving you alone with these guys. No knowing what they want to do to you. Don't ask me to do that."

"If you go alone they'll just think that you thought it was all too much and just left. If you take me with you then they'll know that you're helping me."

"So what? I am helping you. We'll get the cops, or your brothers and we'll get them dealt with." Banner shrugged. "Either way, I'm not leaving you here alone."

"Banner, if you take me out of there, while they plot their next move they're also going to move on to the next girl on their list and they'll be worse to her than they were to me because they'll be even more pissed off." She tried to reason with him. As much as she wanted to let him rescue her, she couldn't let another girl take her place and increase the destruction of lives that these creeps succeeded in. Not if she could help it.

"Well, who's to say that they'd even get to the next girl before we could get here with help? You can't risk yourself like this for someone you don't even know." He countered. "Steff, no stranger is worth that kind of sacrifice."

"I don't know her, but I know her brother and he's a good man. He's a man who would do anything he could to keep her safe from this kind of torment, even if it meant leaving another girl to face it so that he could get help without being hunted down."

He sat down next to her and a sliver of light from outside showed Steff the conflict on Banner's face. He didn't want to do this, to leave her behind, and that was honorable of him, but to take her with him was to condemn his sister to this and worse.

"I can survive this. I can stay strong if I know that you're going to go get my brothers and bring them here to deal with this. You go straight to Nashville, to the bar called The Court, and show them that video. Then you'll bring them here."

"What about the cops? Shouldn't I call them too?" Banner asked.

"My brothers can explain to you why we don't call 911. You just have to promise me that you won't. Just go get my brothers, and Ox. Tell him that I left Dean in Boston and he'll know that I sent you, might save your life."

"They can't be that scary, can they? I don't want to leave you here Steff and I'll never forgive myself for bringing you back here where they could get their hands on you. I'm sorry, and that's why I'll do what you want me to. You gotta know, if I thought I could pull it off I'd just take them out tonight and drive you home myself, but I think this is already bigger than the six of them."

"I think you're right and I think you have to get out of here before they get too quiet up in the house and hear you leave." Steff said, trying to sound braver than she felt.

"Alright. Dammit. I'll go." He ran a hand through his hair. "If you get free somehow, the next farm down the road is a friend of mine and I'll leave a boot knife by the back door for you to get your hands on.

"Just go Banner, get out of here and get back soon."

She watched him leave out the back and lay back down on the grubby mattress. This had to work.

"Please god, let him get to Nashville." She whispered aloud when, several minutes later, she faintly heard his bike engine come to life near the highway. "And don't let Colt kill him when he gets there."

To Be Continued in The Dukes of Hell Book 3: Ox

(I hope the readers will understand how this story, as dark as it is, changed the sequence of whose stories were told. Colt will get his book soon, but Ox needs his chance.)

<u>About the Author</u>

Born in Hardisty, Alberta Monica developed an undeniable love of reading at an early age. Homeschooled during her primary years, her mother not only taught the basics to her five children, but she also read to them at least twice a day. From Anne of Green Gables to Tolkien's Lord of the Rings the stories and the people behind them instilled a love of the written word.

As soon as she could hold a pencil Monica began to write her own stories. Her first complete work was 'Monkey Millionaires' in which a pair of monkeys became millionaires by selling ice cream. While it was a huge hit among the kids in the neighborhood it was just the beginning. After discovering the TV show Spartacus, and full immersion into that fandom, Monica was disappointed to find there was very little fiction to satisfy her desire to indulge a love of Roman era romance. The spark was then lit to write the stories she wanted to read herself.

Despite some eye-opening experiences (it's not as glamorous a profession as the movies would have you believe) she would not change her journey in the slightest. When she is not working or writing, Monica is a single parent to a little girl. Nothing makes her happier than when her daughter tells her that she wants to be a writer, "Just like you, Mommy." So, to keep inspiring a very special little girl, and to bring some elements of romantic Rome and the romance of real life to some not-so-little girls, she is pleased to be writing as M. Francis Lamont and brings you "The Champion's Prize" the first of her centurion saga and many more stories to come. She encourages everyone to "Live with Passion. Live with Purpose. And most important of all, Never Lose."

Welcome to the beginning of something wonderful.